For Benedicte Barford and Stephanie Amster
with love and thanks Emma

ORCHARD BOOKS

338 Euston Road, London NW1 3BH

Orchard Books Australia

Level 17/207 Kent Street, Sydney, NSW 2000

First published as *I Don't Want a Cool Cat*
in 2009 by Orchard Books
This edition first published in 2014

ISBN 9781408331255

A CIP catalogue record for this book
is available from the British Library.

1 3 5 7 9 10 8 6 4 2

Printed in China

Orchard Books is a division of
Hachette Children's Books,
an Hachette UK company.
www.hachette.co.uk

I love cats

Emma
Dodd

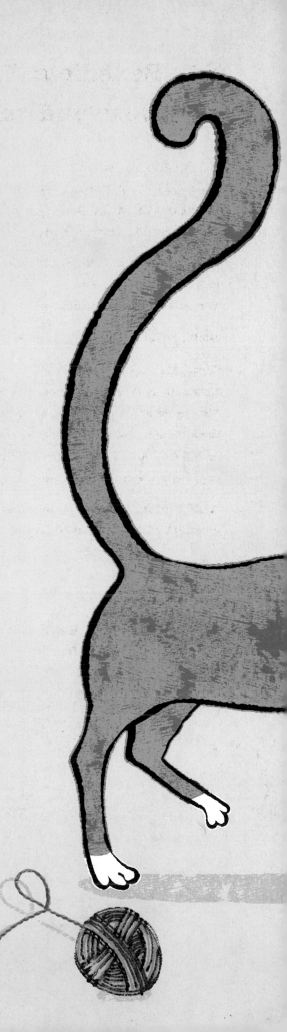

ORCHARD

I love all cats,
Big . . .

. . . and small cats.

I love huffy cats,

Puffy, ball-of-fluffy cats.

I even love
night cats,

Out looking-for-a-fight cats.

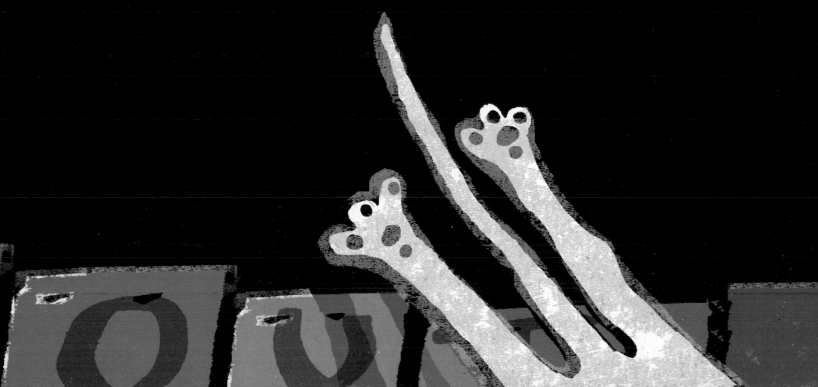

I love greedy cats,

Miaow-miaow-please-feed-me cats.

I love prize cats,

The best-that-money-buys cats.

I love prowly cats,

Howly, scowly, yowly cats.

I love
brave
cats . . .

... and

not-so-well-behaved

cats.

But my
best cat
is a
purry
cat.

A small,
soft,
furry cat.

Not a scratch-or-scrap cat.
A curl-up-in-my-lap cat.

A glad-

when-I-

come-home

cat . . .

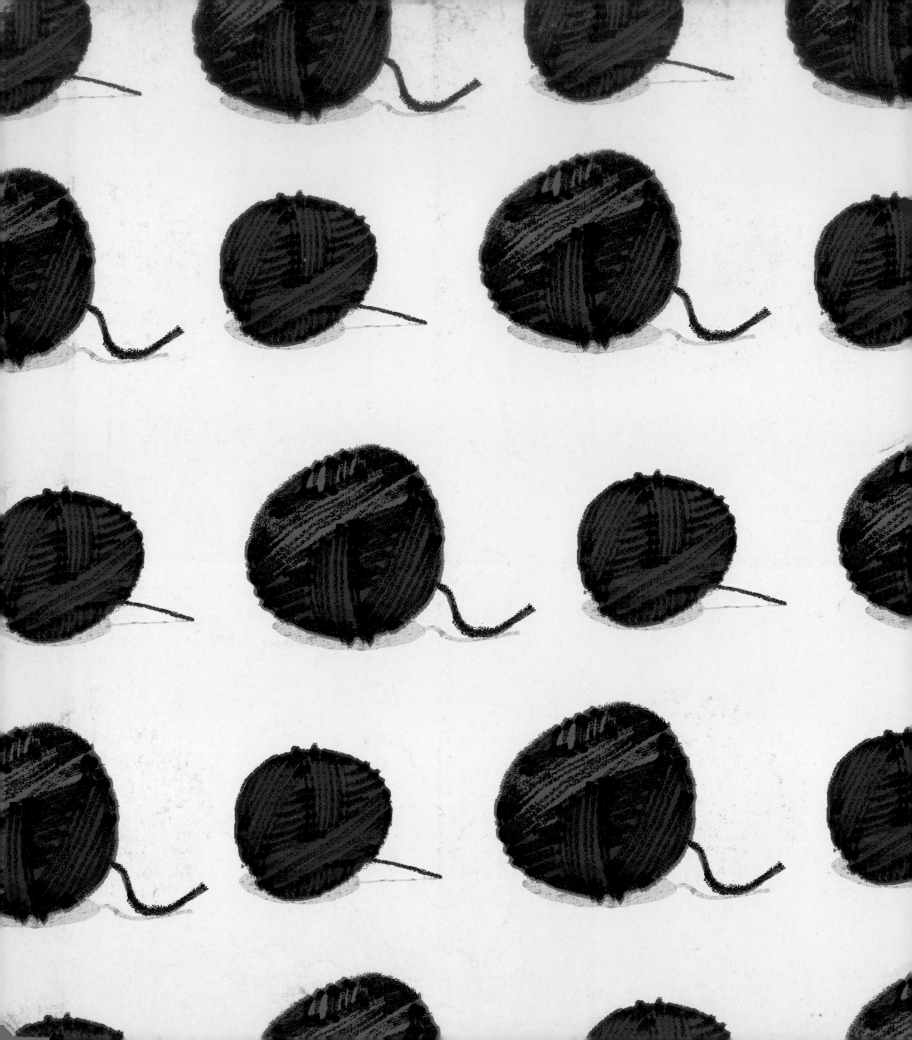